Animal Adventure

Written by Christine Ricci
Illustrated by Dave Aikins, Tom Mangano, and Victoria Miller

Louis Weber, C.E.O.
Publications International, Ltd.
7373 North Cicero Avenue, Lincolnwood, Illinois 60712
Ground Floor, 59 Gloucester Place, London W1U 8JJ

Customer Service: 1-800-595-8484 or customer__service@pilbooks.com

www.pilbooks.com

8 7 6 5 4 3 2 1

ISBN-13: 978-1-4127-8922-6
ISBN-10: 1-4127-8922-2

publications international, ltd.

¡Hola! I'm Dora. My puppy, Perrito, is waiting for me at my house. I have to get home to feed and walk him. We need to find the quickest way to my house. Let's check Map. Map says that the quickest way to my house is down the Lazy River and through the Rainbow Rainforest.

Look! It's Baby Blue Bird! She looks lost!
We have to help her find her home.

Where does a bird live? A nest!
Do you see a nest? Right, in the tree!
Let's help Baby Blue Bird get back in
her tree, safe and sound.

Now we have to get to the Lazy River.
Aw, that little turtle is upside down and
can't turn himself over. Let's help him! We
have to be gentle so he doesn't get scared.

Will you help me turn him over? Great! Now let's take this little turtle to the Lazy River. Do you see the river? There it is! C'mon, little turtle, follow me!

The little turtle sure is happy to be back home! Now look at all the other animals who live in or near the Lazy River!

There are 5 frogs, 4 turtles, 3 ducks, 2 fish, and 1 snake! We don't want to bump into any of the animals so we need to go slow! *¡Despacio!* Yay! We went slow and kept the animals safe!

We made it down the Lazy River! Hey! Look at that goat! What is he eating? Yes, it's a sock! Socks aren't food! Eating the sock could make that goat sick.

We want to keep all animals safe,
so let's help the goat eat healthy
food. Will you check my backpack for
a carrot? Great!

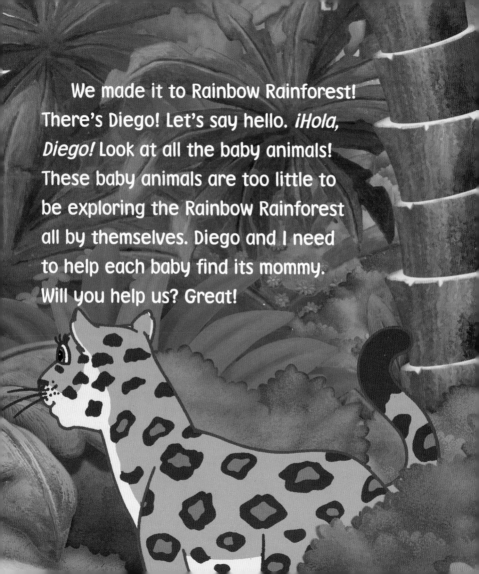

We made it to Rainbow Rainforest! There's Diego! Let's say hello. *¡Hola, Diego!* Look at all the baby animals! These baby animals are too little to be exploring the Rainbow Rainforest all by themselves. Diego and I need to help each baby find its mommy. Will you help us? Great!

I'm glad we helped all those baby animals get back to their parents! Baby animals should be taken care of. Here's my house! And here comes Perrito! I'm so happy to see Perrito! And he's happy to see me! He's giving me kisses! I love getting kisses! Do you?

C'mon, Perrito! Let's go for a walk! Puppies need their exercise! Look! All the animals we helped keep safe today want to thank us! You're welcome, little animals! And thank you for helping me take care of all these animals today! We did it!